For Tom, the sweetest
little monster in town ~ S.P-H. x

For Jason ~ A.R.

Bloomsbury Publishing, London, New Delhi, New York and Sydney

First published in Great Britain in 2014 by Bloomsbury Publishing Plc
50 Bedford Square, London, WC1B 3DP

Text copyright © Smriti Prasadam-Halls 2014
Illustrations copyright © Angela Rozelaar 2014

The moral rights of the author and illustrator have been asserted

A CIP catalogue record for this book is available from the British Library

ISBN 978 1 4088 3881 5 (HB)
ISBN 978 1 4088 3882 2 (PB)
ISBN 978 1 4088 4618 6 (eBook)

Printed in China by C & C Offset Printing Co Ltd, Shenzhen, Guangdong

1 3 5 7 9 10 8 6 4 2

www.bloomsbury.com

All papers used by Bloomsbury Publishing are natural, recyclable products made from
wood grown in well-managed forests. The manufacturing processes conform
to the environmental regulations of the country of origin

Smriti Prasadam-Halls   Angie Rozelaar

Don't Call Me Sweet!

BLOOMSBURY

LONDON   NEW DELHI   NEW YORK   SYDNEY

I'm a giant monster,
with sharp, sharp claws.
I've got big, spiky teeth
and loud, loud roars.

RAAAAH!

Which is why I say,
to everyone I meet...
CALL ME SCARY...

...don't call me SWEET!

When I'm practising
monster moves,

STOMP,

STOMP,

STOMP!

If, by accident,
I fall into the swamp,
I'll be covered in mud
from my head to my feet....

. . . so call me STINKY. Don't call me SWEET!

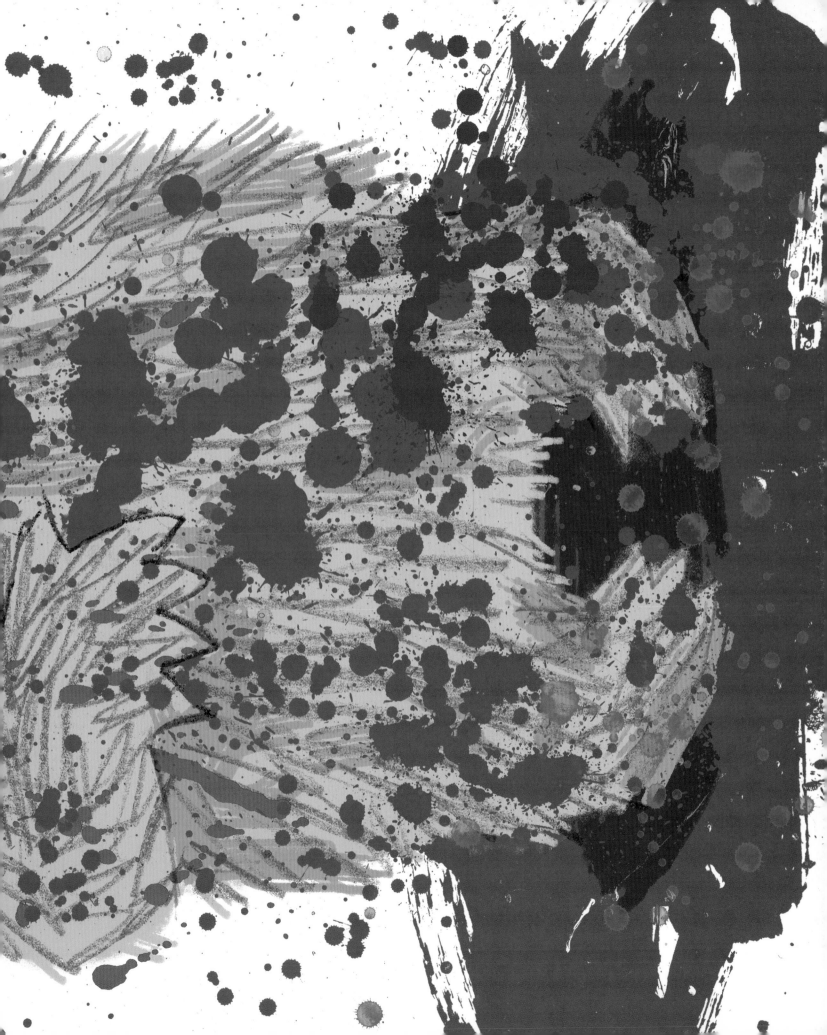

When I make a great big mess,
cooking bug eye stew,

And my hair and tail
and claws get
splattered with goo,

Don't pat my head as **I** come slipping down the street . . .

Call me
SLIMY,
don't call me
SWEET!

I'm a stinky, slimy monster,
with a scary monster face.
Look out, here I come - RAAH!
I'm ready for a chase.

I'm out to terrify anyone I meet.
So you'd better call me **SCARY**.
Don't call me . . .

AAAAAGH! It's an ogre
and he's looking down at me!
If he catches me now,
He'll eat me for his tea.

He's massive and he's mean,
I think he weighs a tonne,
Oh no, there's nothing for it,
I think I'd better RUN!

"Stop!" growls the ogre.
"Now what have we here?
Why, the yummiest
looking monster
that I've seen all year.
Scary . . . stinky . . . slimy . . .
ooh, a tasty teatime treat.

You look just the
type of monster
that I LOVE
to EAT!"

Who me? **I** squeak politely,

Oooh, **I'M** not scary.
I'm not stinky or slimy
or even big and hairy

No, I'm the nicest monster
that you could **EVER** meet.
So please don't call me scary,
because **I'm** just rather . . .